11/2021

To all the hardworking delivery people,
who do their best every day
—D. R.

To all the people who still send cards,
postcards, and presents to their beloved ones
—B. M.

SIMON SPOTLIGHT
An imprint of Simon & Schuster Children's Publishing Division
1230 Avenue of the Americas, New York, New York 10020
This Simon Spotlight edition August 2021
Text copyright © 2021 by Dana Regan
Illustrations copyright © 2021 by Berta Maluenda
SIMON SPOTLIGHT, READY-TO-READ, and colophon are registered
trademarks of Simon & Schuster, Inc.
For information about special discounts for bulk purchases, please contact
Simon & Schuster Special Sales at 1-866-506-1949 or
business@simonandschuster.com.
Manufactured in the United States of America 0721 LAK
10 9 8 7 6 5 4 3 2 1
Cataloging-in-Publication Data for this book is available from the
Library of Congress.
ISBN 978-1-5344-8907-3 (hc)
ISBN 978-1-5344-8906-6 (pbk)
ISBN 978-1-5344-8908-0 (ebook)

The Big Mix-Up!

by Dana Regan · illustrated by Berta Maluenda

Ready-to-Read

Simon Spotlight

New York   London   Toronto   Sydney   New Delhi

This is Mike, and
Mike delivers,

in the town of
Happy Rivers.

You order things
from any store,

and Mike will bring
them to your door.

His list is long
and hard to read,

but Mike can bring
you what you need.

But Mike began to
stress and worry.

Even close,
his list was blurry.

Mar ordered hats.
Mike brings her cats.

Jay needs a fan.

Mike brings a pan.

Raj paid for pens.
Mike brings him hens.

Dan wanted pants.
Mike gave him ants.

Ted asked for wigs.

Mike brings him pigs.

Mike does not like
to make mistakes.

He thought for sure the list said snakes!

Mike calls Doc Wells.
Mike cannot see.

The doctor says,
"Come visit me."

Doc Wells asks Mike
to read the chart.

Mike cannot see
the lower part.

New glasses help!

Now Mike can see!

He sees each leaf
on every tree.

So now when Cole
asks for a sled,

Mike will not bring
a bed instead.

His friends all cheer,
"We're proud of you!"

They like his cool
new glasses, too!

This is Mike, and
Mike delivers,
in the town of
Happy Rivers.

You order things
from any store,

and Mike will bring them
to your door.